≈ ≈ ≈ ≈ ≈ ≈

"But I have to ask one more time: Are you sure you're ready?" Brandie said. "Because I don't want to be simply your first time. When I make love to a woman, I do it because she's the woman I want to be with."

"I want to be with you, too," Angela said. And she meant it. She never slept with anyone just for the sex. She was thrilled about being in a relationship with Brandie, and she knew the lovemaking would deepen their bond.

Brandie reached and brushed the hairs away from Angela's face. She leaned forward and kissed her softly. She suckled Angela's bottom lip and pulled it slightly with her teeth. The contact was brief, but Angela felt the impact like a kick to the chest. A tingling heat radiated down her legs, to her toes and then back up again. It came to a rest around her clitoris and began to throb pleasantly.

Brandie backed away and drank the rest of her wine. She placed the glass on the coffee table and slowly rose to her feet. She walked away without a word. Angela was hesitant to follow, but Brandie removed her robe just as she disappeared down the hallway. Angela's eyes widened. She didn't have time to see if Brandie had anything on beneath the robe. Angela stared at the discarded garment for a few seconds and then quickly finished her second drink. She placed the wineglass on the table and stood uneasily.

The slight friction her thighs created as she followed was tantalizing. Angela's heart thundered. She took a deep breath and tried to calm herself when she reached the hallway. Brandie was nowhere in sight, but there was an open bedroom door ahead on the left. Angela's heels sank in the plush carpet as she moved in that direction.

≈ ≈ ≈ ≈ ≈ ≈

MIGHT BE BI PART ONE

MIGHT BE BI

A NOVELLA

PART ONE
CURIOUS

I0589154

KEITH THOMAS WALKER

KEITHWALKERBOOKS, INC
This is a UMS production

KEITHWALKERBOOKS

Publishing Company
KeithWalkerBooks, Inc.
P.O. Box 331585
Fort Worth, TX 76163

For information write
KeithWalkerBooks, Inc.
P.O. Box 331585
Fort Worth, TX 76163

ISBN-13 DIGIT: 978-0-9850500-5-4
ISBN-10 DIGIT: 0985050055
Library of Congress Control Number: 2013909362
Manufactured in the United States of America

First Edition

Visit us at www.keithwalkerbooks.com

KEITH THOMAS WALKER

This book is for Sharon Blount
President of B.R.A.B. Book Club

MORE BOOKS BY
KEITH THOMAS WALKER

Fixin' Tyrone
How to Kill Your Husband
A Good Dude
Riding the Corporate Ladder
The Finley Sisters' Oath of Romance
Blow by Blow
Jewell and the Dapper Dan
Harlot
Plan C (And More KWB Shorts)
Dripping Chocolate
The Realest Ever
Jackson Memorial

Visit keithwalkerbooks.com for information
about these and upcoming titles from
KeithWalkerBooks

ACKNOWLEGMENTS

Of course I would like to thank God, first and foremost, for giving me the creativity and drive to pursue my dreams and the understanding that I am nothing without Him. I would like to thank my wife for being my first and most important critic, and I would like to thank my mother for always pushing me to be the best I can be. I would like to thank Janae Hafford-Hampton for being the best advisor, supporter and little sister a brother could ever have. I would also like to thank (in no particular order) Brandy Rees, Denise Bolds, Sabrina Scott, Dianne Guinn, Kierra Pease, Cathy Atchison, Jason Owens, Sharon Blount, BRAB Book Club, Trey Williams and Uncle Steven Thomas, one love. I'd like to thank everyone who purchased and enjoyed one of my books. Everything I do has always been to please you! I know there are folks who mean the world to me that I'm failing to mention. I apologize ahead of time. Rest assured I'm grateful for everything you've done for me!

MIGHT BE BI PART ONE

CHAPTER ONE
MIGHT BE

"You might be what?" Keshaun asked.

"I said I might be bi."

"Bi *what*?"

Angela frowned. "What you think?"

"Bi-*sexual*?" Keshaun asked.

Angela looked around the gym. No one was paying them any attention, but she rolled her eyes before responding. "That's what I said."

Keshaun grinned. His teeth were nice and white, in contrast to his dark brown skin.

Angela grinned, too, and she had to look away from him.

The 24 Hour Fitness center was filled with its usual Friday night crowd. There were men and women sweating it out on the treadmills, exercise bikes and with weights. Some wanted to get in shape so they could do something different on Friday nights, preferably something with the opposite sex. Others already had the physiques they wanted, and they were there to tone their beautifully sculpted muscles. A couple of remarkably fit guys were on the prowl, hoping to pick up a client or two for their own personal training class.

It was seven pm on what had been a beautiful spring day in Overbrook Meadows, Texas. Angela spent the afternoon trying to get a foreign couple into a ridiculously gaudy McMansion on the west side of town. The house had been on the market for over a year, and everyone at Angela's real estate office had a shot at it. If Angela managed to sell the place, her colleagues would put her on a pedestal for the rest of the year – not to mention the huge commission she'd get for closing the deal.

Keshaun worked as a nurse at Jackson Memorial. He got off at seven am and entertained a female friend who had been waiting at his home. He didn't get to sleep until eleven. He woke up fresh and energized at six pm and hurried to meet Angela at the gym. Because of his abnormal sleep schedule, he was sure to be up until the wee hours of the morning. But such was the curse of the third-shift worker. He was used to it by now.

Angela and Keshaun sat on a mat together with their legs spread and the soles of their shoes touching. They both had athletic builds, and they knew to stretch diligently before each workout. Angela missed both of her other gym days this week and planned to make up for it tonight. An hour on the elliptical machine sounded like a good start. She bent at the hips and reached for her right foot, stretching her back and hamstrings.

Keshaun held her hands while she stretched in the middle, before reaching for her left foot. He then crossed his legs Indian-style, still grinning as he watched her. Angela smirked at him, and she crossed her legs, too.

"You ain't gay," Keshaun said.

Of course he would know. They were besties now, but there was a time when Angela couldn't keep her hands off him. He was still a nice hunk of a man. Keshaun was tall and as dark as the night itself. He had the slender, yet muscular build of a swimmer. Keshaun kept his hair short and never wore a moustache or beard. His hands were big, and his feet were big, and Angela knew for a fact that his third leg was up to par. Tonight he wore basketball shorts with low top sneakers and a tee-shirt with the sleeves ripped off. His arm muscles were perfectly toned. His biceps were massive.

Angela wore black yoga pants with a big, unflattering tee-shirt that hung well past her butt. But she was a classic beauty, regardless of how she tried to downplay it. Angela was mocha-colored with a slim waist, a flat stomach and a pair of the best-looking natural breasts Keshaun had ever seen. She was of average height with slender legs and nice hips that looked awesome in jeans and evening gowns. Angela preferred to go to the gym with her best bud, because no one hit on her when Keshaun was around. Even hardcore bodybuilders were intimidated by him.

11

"I didn't say I was gay," she replied. "I said I think I might be bi-sexual."

"All I asked was why you broke up with Calvin," Keshaun said. "I know you ain't saying—"

"That is what I'm saying," Angela said. "I think that's why."

Keshaun's mouth hung open. He had known Angela for nearly a decade, since they met during his first and her last year at Texas Lutheran University. He had witnessed her sexuality first hand, and he knew of a string of relationships Angela had – *all with men* – since they broke up. His friend might be a lot of things, but anti-dick was not one of them. He shook his head.

"Naw, I don't see that at all. Don't get me wrong, I want to see it. Shit, I'll pay money to see it!"

Angela laughed and shook her head. "Pervert."

"You don't like women, Angie," Keshaun continued. "I never seen anything like that in you, not as long as I've known you. What that nigga do to you? You want me to whoop his ass?"

Angela got up and headed for her punishment. Keshaun hopped up, too.

"Where you going," he asked. "The elliptical?"

"I have to," Angela said. "If this is my only workout for the week, I gotta make it count."

"We can come back tomorrow night," Keshaun said. "I'm off this weekend."

"I got a date tomorrow night," Angela said.

"With who?" Keshaun asked. "How long you been broke up with Calvin?"

"It's been two months."

"But you said y'all went out a couple of weeks ago," Keshaun recalled, still following her.

"He's been trying to get back with me ever since we broke up," Angela explained. "I did go out with him a few times, but it just... There was nothing there. We stopped having sex about a month before we broke up."

Keshaun grabbed her hand. "Come on, Angie, let's get on the exercise bikes, so we can talk."

"No, I need to get on this bad boy here," Angela said. She placed a hand on the unforgiving machine.

"We can get on the bikes," Keshaun said. "The ones with the moving handles. It's the same thing."

"No it's not."

"Come on," Keshaun pleaded. "You need to holler at me. How you gon' tell me you wanna be with a girl and then come way over here to work out by yourself? If you wanna kiss on girls and stuff, I need to know about it."

"Alright," Angela conceded. "Come on." She turned and headed for the exercise bikes instead.

"That is what you're talking about, right?" Keshaun asked as he walked with her. "You said you wanna kiss on girls?" His smile was absolutely devilish.

"I can probably find someone *more mature* to talk to about this," Angela said, but she was smiling, too.

"No, I think if you wanna talk about something like that, you should talk to an expert," Keshaun replied.

"How are you an expert?" Angela wondered. "Are you gay?"

"Hell no. I'm talking about being an expert on kissing girls."

"I never knew *expert* and *whore* meant the same thing."

"When it's a man, it's an expert. When it's a woman, it's a whore," Keshaun explained. "That's one double-standard we need to keep alive and kicking!"

≈≈≈≈≈≈

The friends met in a religion class at Texas Lutheran University in 2004. They came together due to a mutual despise for their haughty professor and hit it off well as study partners. Within a month of meeting each other, Angela found herself waiting for Keshaun after her last class for the day. He would pull up to her dorm and whisk her away in his Cutlass Supreme, which had 20 inch rims and bone rattling woofers in the trunk.

The thing Angela found most intriguing about Keshaun was the dual lives he seemed to lead. At school he was quiet and seldom seen, rarely hanging out with his peers in the student union building or the cafeteria. Outside of school Keshaun was one with the streets. He lived in a cheap one bedroom apartment on the south side of town. He sold marijuana all the way through college and smoked a good deal of his supply along the way. Keshaun wore baggy Dickey pants and flannel jackets in the wintertime, and his car had a prominent bullet hole in the passenger door. A lot of students were afraid of him. Angela was drawn to him, but not because she craved a hoodlum.

What Angela found so sexy about Keshaun was his brain. He completed two years of community college before transferring to Texas Lutheran. He had a couple of years to go on his nursing degree, and he aced every test in their religion class. Keshaun had a lot of knuckleheaded tendencies, but he was determined to finish what he started.

He once told Angela, "College kids think they're smart because they can memorize a bunch of stuff. That's not smart. A parrot can do that. But when a *real* smart cat like me figure out he can memorize just like them, then there ain't no boundaries. I went to school because I wanted to, and I do good at it because I can. Why you think this college let a nigga like me up in here? I made straight A's when I was getting my associates. They begged me to come here. Gave me a full ride."

Angela couldn't get her panties off fast enough.

The sex with Keshaun was as wild and untamed as he was, but it was also their undoing. Angela was so sprung, she fell into a daze many times thinking about Keshaun's dick. That wasn't so bad until it started to happen while she was at school. Angela bombed two tests in a row in separate classes and had to give Keshaun his walking papers. Her aunt Gayle warned her to never make a fool of herself over a man. Angela was in her last year of college. She made it this far without getting dick-whipped, and as fine and perplexing as Keshaun was, she knew he wasn't the only or the last man in the world.

She gave him the old *Let's still be friends* routine, and Keshaun surprised her by hunting her down every chance he got, to make sure Angela lived up to that promise. That's the way she liked to remember it. Keshaun hounded her. He started hanging around after class so he could have lunch or go study with Angela. That was fine, but she wouldn't leave the campus with him. After awhile, he stopped asking and became a true study buddy. Gradually Keshaun became a bigger presence on the campus, and Angela believed she brought him out of his shell. She hated to leave him when she graduated the following year.

Since then, they had been there for each other for everything from boyfriend/girlfriend trouble to the death of Keshaun's brother and Angela's cancer scare six years ago. She cried on Keshaun's shoulder when the doctor told her they could only beat the cancer by taking away any hope of her having a child.

Angela and Keshaun had sex exactly *once* since college. It was after a company Christmas party at one of Keshaun's colleague's homes. They got so drunk, they had to take a cab when the party shut down at 3 am. Somehow they ended up in Angela's bed, laughing and ripping off clothes like the good old days. Fortunately Angela became nauseous a few seconds after penetration, and she couldn't make it out of bed before the contents of her stomach made a reverse trip.

They both grimaced in the shower as they washed the vomit off, and Angela declared that the ultimate omen. Obviously they were definitely meant to be friends ONLY. Keshaun never let on how disappointed he was over the botched opportunity to feel Angela's sweet, pink walls again.

≈ ≈ ≈ ≈ ≈ ≈

They took a seat on stationary bikes that were a few feet apart, facing a wall-to-wall mirror. There were several television monitors above head, but Keshaun couldn't take his eyes off Angela as she adjusted the settings on her bike. She looked up at the mirror and caught him gawking.

"Is that what you're gonna do?" she asked. "Start acting like a pervert?"

"Stop saying that," Keshaun replied. "I'm just in awe about what you said, not a pervert."

"Yeah, I'm sure you are. Just like any other man; y'all fantasize about this stuff."

"Seems to me you the one been fantasizing about it," Keshaun said. He grinned when he saw Angela trying to suppress a giggle. "Tell me about it," he said as he climbed onto his own bike. "Start with Calvin. What went wrong with y'all?"

Angela got her legs moving, which caused the handles of the bike to move as well. It wasn't as engrossing as the elliptical machine, but the workout could be demanding, depending on how long and how hard she pushed herself. She looked up at the mirror and frowned at Keshaun who was still watching her reflection. Angela had her shoulder-length hair pulled back in a ponytail. Even with the make-up free look she wore to the gym, she was very attractive.

"He asked me to marry him," Angela said.

"When?" Keshaun asked. "Why didn't you tell me?"

"Because I didn't know what was wrong with me," Angela said. "I told you he asked me to move in with him. You remember? It was at the same time. I didn't know why I didn't want to go."

"Yeah. But you didn't say he wanted to marry you, too."

Angela shook her head. "I guess I was kinda freaked out about it."

"I remember," Keshaun said. "I thought you was just nervous because you never had a serious relationship like that. You said you were gonna think about it. I told you to go. Calvin gets paid. You would've been living real nice. And you been with him for over a year. You said you loved him."

"I did," Angela said. "That's why I didn't know what was wrong with me. Calvin was perfect. We had dreams together. I just had to take one step to make it all come true, but I couldn't do it. I backed out. I was scared."

"Scared of what?"

"I was scared because I knew it wasn't what I really wanted. I wasn't a hundred percent satisfied with Calvin. He was always there for me, but it wasn't enough. There was something he couldn't give me. I didn't know what it was. I just..." She shrugged. "I started to get real bored."

"*Bored*? He wasn't putting it down in the bedroom?" Keshaun asked.

Angela shook her head. "He tried."

"You wouldn't have stayed with him for that long if he wasn't doing it right," Keshaun reasoned.

"That's the thing. He was doing it right. He was switching it up, trying new stuff. He made me feel good. But it just... It wasn't enough."

Angela met Keshaun's eyes in the mirror. He had that stupid look again.

"Ay, you know your boy over here could–"

"Shut up."

"Naw, I'm just saying..." Keshaun smiled broadly. "You know I can knock the dust off that thang, like we did back in–"

"Ugh!" Angela gagged.

"What?"

"I'ma throw up," she said. She covered her mouth with one hand. "You gon' make me throw up. Just thinking about it is getting me sick!"

Keshaun smacked his lips. "Whatever, girl. How long you gon' keep bringing that up? You know it didn't have nothing to do with me. That was you and all them goddamned margaritas. Guzzling 'em like they was finna run out."

"Either way," Angela said. "All I know is I will *never* go there with you again. Anyway, this isn't even about you, ol' big-headed boy. Can't you just–"

"Yeah, I got a *big head*," Keshaun said. "And you know it can make all of your troubles go away, if you..." He trailed off because of the look on Angela's face.

"Alright, man," she snarled. "Whatever. Leave me alone."

"I'm sorry. I was just playing."

"This ain't a time for playing, Keshaun. I'm trying to talk to you about something serious. Why you always wanna go there? Are you horny? Where your woman at? Aren't you still with Deena?"

"I ain't really *with* her with her."

Keshaun had been in an on-again-off-again relationship with a lawyer for more than a decade. She was the main catalyst in his decision to enroll in college and make something of himself. Keshaun was tired of Deena always looking down her nose at him, though he would never admit it.

"I said I was just playing," Keshaun said, and he tried to get back on topic. "So you feel like whatever's missing in your life is a woman?" It was hard, but he managed to say it with a straight face.

Angela took a deep breath. This was the first time she told anyone about her secret desires.

"I've been feeling like this for a long time."

Keshaun watched her eyes in the mirror. He had never seen her look so sincere.

"Feeling like you're, um, gay?"

Angela shook her head. "No. I can't be. You know I love me some dick."

Keshaun wiped his smile away when Angela flared her nostrils as a warning.

"But you might be bi-sexual?" he asked.

"Yeah." Angela nodded. "I'm definitely curious."

Keshaun stared at her. He was truly astounded. "That's... That's... I never would've thought that was anywhere near your radar."

"I have a gay aunt," Angela said.

"Gayle," Keshaun said. "I know. You told me about her."

"Yeah, but I didn't tell you that when I was little, I wanted to be like her. Everybody in the family used to talk about her, behind her back. There was always so much whispering going on when she came to the family reunions and stuff. When I finally

21

found out what the big secret was, I was fascinated." Angela's eyes lit up at the memory. "I never knew that a woman could be with another woman. From the moment I learned that it was possible, it's been something I wanted to do."

Keshaun swallowed. His throat was completely dry. "Why you, why you wait so long?" he asked. Angela would be thirty-four on her next birthday.

"Because when I started having sex," she said, "I fell in love with men." Angela had a sudden twinkle in her eyes. "I love every aspect of sex with a man. My thoughts about being with a woman started to recede, and after a while I didn't even think about it anymore. But every now and then it would flare up again. I'd be on the verge of acting on it, and then I'd chicken out. But this last time, when I started getting those cravings, it was real strong. And it's still burning. I haven't had sex in three months. I lost all desire to be with Calvin."

"Maybe it's just a dry spell," Keshaun guessed. "You'll be alright when you meet a new man."

"I don't want to meet a new man," Angela insisted. "I want to be with a woman, and I'm going to do it. Everything in my life is lined up perfectly right now. I'm not going to be married with kids one day wondering *what if.*"

"So what are you gonna do?" Keshaun asked.

"I'm going out with a woman," Angela told him. "Tomorrow."

"Seriously?"

"Her name is Brandie," Angela said. "She went to college with us."

Keshaun's eyes widened. "Whoa! I remember her!" He put a hand over his open mouth. "I heard she was gay!"

Angela frowned as she looked around. "Could you shut the hell up?"

"Oh, shit. My bad," Keshaun said, and he lowered his voice. "You still keep in touch with her?"

Angela shook her head. "Nope. I ran into her at Starbucks today."

"She asked you out?"

"No. Brandie would never come on to me – not after what happened in college."

"Wh, what happened in college?" Keshaun asked. He had to squeeze his lips together to keep from grinning.

Angela laughed at the expression he made. "She came on to me."

Keshaun's eyes fluttered as he sighed. "Okay, you gotta let me fantasize about that for at least a second." He closed his eyes and hummed. "Man, Brandie was real pretty. Too skinny, but that face, and them titties. Hmph. She was real nice."

"She's not skinny anymore," Angela informed him. "She filled out nicely. *Real nice*." She had the same dreamy look in her eyes that Keshaun had.

"This is some crazy shit."

Angela nodded. "It is."

"What'd y'all do in college?" Keshaun asked. "You said she came on to you?"

"She was my roommate when I was a freshman," Angela said. "She had to move out after that first year, but we got really close."

Keshaun's perverted grin was back. "Do tell."

Angela rolled her eyes at him. "I knew Brandie was gay, and, I don't know... You know she was pretty. I was definitely attracted to her. After a while, I think I started flirting with her."

Keshaun's chest rose and fell slowly as he pedaled his bike. He tried his best to get rid of a slight boner that was growing gradually.

"When she kissed me—"

"She kissed you?"

"Yes," Angela said. "But I got scared and took off, and it was never the same with us. When she moved out of the dorm, we had even less reason to come in contact with each other. I know she avoided me for the next three years because she was embarrassed, and I avoided her for the same reason."

"You never told me y'all were that close," Keshaun noted.

"Sometimes people who have feelings for the same sex keep a lot of secrets," Angela said wistfully. "Haven't you ever done anything, with a boy, that you never told anyone?"

Keshaun's face scrunched up. "Ewww. Hell naw."

"I had a boyfriend who touched penises with his cousin," Angela recalled, "when they were in grade school. He never told anyone about it, except me."

Keshaun was clearly disgusted. "He shoulda took that secret all the way to the grave. Did you still like him, after he told you that?"

Angela chuckled. "Of course I did. He wasn't gay. He just didn't know what to do with his dick back then. He didn't know anything about sex. I think I liked him even more because he trusted me enough to tell his secret. I know I had plenty of secrets, about my sexuality."

"But you're not keeping secrets no more?"

"I didn't say that."

"But you are going out with a girl tomorrow, like a real date?"

"Well, yeah, for me it will be. But I don't think Brandie knows that. I just told her we should get together to catch up."

"Where y'all going?"

"To Pappadeaux."

"What are you gonna do?" Keshaun asked, "reach across the table and hold her hand. Give her one of those winks? You know what I'm talking about..."

Angela grinned. "I, honestly I don't know what I'm going to do."

"But you still like her?"

Angela nodded. "Ever since college." She was sweating and getting a little winded now.

"Damn. Can I go?"

"Sorry. Three's a crowd."

"Would you, will you take a picture of her?" Keshaun asked. "I wanna see what she looks like now. You say she filled out nicely? She got a fat ass?"

"It's bigger than mine."

"And you wanna grab it, huh?" Keshaun still couldn't believe this was happening, but loved being part of the discussion.

Angela nodded. "I do wanna grab it. I really do."

"When you, um, when you get back, can I smell your finger?"

Angela shook her head at him for the last time, and she hopped off her bike.

"I'm through with you." She threw a towel at his face before she walked away.

Keshaun laughed and wiped the sweat off his mug until Angela told him, "I don't know whose towel that is."

"Ewww! Man, what the fuck?" He threw it back at her angrily.

Angela caught the towel and laughed at him. "It's my towel, pervert."

CHAPTER TWO
BRANDIE

Twelve years ago Brandie was one of the first people Angela met when she began her freshman year at Texas Lutheran University. College was not an immediate concern for Angela when she graduated from Finley High School. She hadn't figured out what she wanted to do with the rest of her life by her senior year, and she didn't take her parents advice about at least getting her pre-requisites out of the way as soon as possible.

Instead Angela took a three year vacation that gradually turned into an adult-world struggle when her parents stopped financing her carefree lifestyle. After working a dead-end job for more than a year, Angela decided she was ready to go to college as a finance major. Her parents were thrilled to hear that and had no problem funding her higher education.

Brandie was a few years younger than Angela because she enrolled in college right after high school. Brandie was an education major. She came from a poor family, and she was still in shock about making it to a real university. Her dorm room with Angela was the first time she had ever been away from her family for a prolonged period of time. The two girls became fast friends. They didn't have any classes together, but they were joined at the hip at all other times.

Angela was attracted to Brandie from the moment she laid eyes on her. Brandie's skin was dark and beautiful. She had full lips, large eyes and a bright smile that made Angela's heart float every time she saw her. Brandie was a Skinny Minnie back then, but her boobs were awesome. And Angela couldn't stop staring at her ass whenever Brandie pranced around their dorm room in leggings or just panties.

Angela had desires to be with a woman when she was in high school, but they were easily suppressed. Her new roommate brought all of those wants and cravings back to the surface. When Brandie confided in her that she was gay, Angela knew right then that this would be the first woman she made love to. It was destined. Nearly every student at the university tried something wild and new while they were away from their controlling parents. Angela didn't drink, and she certainly wouldn't put anything up her nose, but Brandie gave her goose bumps.

Sometimes, when they stayed up late at night talking, Angela imagined what it would be like if she left her bed and slipped under the sheets with Brandie. She knew it would be a lot different than her encounters with boys. Angela wanted to cuddle with her roommate. She wanted to feel the warmth under

Brandie's covers; the heat of Brandie's dark brown skin against her own. She wanted to place her lips on Brandie's neck and inhale the scents of her body wash, shampoo and her natural pheromones.

Sometimes, when the only faint light in the room came from a street lamp outside of their curtained window, Angela would touch herself. She would listen to Brandie talk about her day, and she would close her eyes and pretend it was Brandie's hand on her rather than her own. She never slipped into full masturbation, but Angela drifted off to sleep with moist panties plenty of times.

Her desire became a yearning, but Angela's fear of crossing the invisible line she had drawn for her sexuality was equally strong. What would happen if the boys at school found out? If she got labeled a *lezzy*, it was sure to follow her through her collegiate career. And Angela would absolutely die if her parents found out. More importantly, Angela didn't think she was a lesbian. She had feelings for women in the past, but they always faded. If she continued to ignore it, she was sure her cravings would fade again.

The incident occurred on April 14th, an unusually rainy day. The university was abuzz with graduation preparations for the seniors and stress-inducing final exams for everyone else. Angela met Brandie in the library after lunch. Through a window on the second floor, they watched the dark clouds gather until they totally blocked out the sun. By the time they were ready to leave, the university had issued a flash flood warning. The roommates dreaded the 300 yard trek to their dorm.

"We're gonna get drenched," Angela said gloomily. She stuffed all of her books in her backpack but worried they might still get wet during the journey.

"At least you have on jeans," Brandie noted. She wore a denim skirt with sandals. She eyed Angela's sneakers with envy.

"Yeah, but you have an umbrella," Angela said.

"You can share it with me," Brandie said right away.

"I already know that," Angela said with a grin. "You think I was going to let you stay dry all by yourself?"

"But look at it," Brandie said, staring out of the window. "It's raining sideways. We'll still get soaked."

"But at least we'll get soaked together."

Brandie smiled back at her.

Angela couldn't help but tell her, "You got pretty lips."

Brandie continued to smile, but she looked away in embarrassment.

"I'm sorry," Angela told her.

"No, it just–"

"I didn't mean anything."

Brandie smirked at her. "No, it's me. You caught me off guard. Usually if I hear something like that from a girl…"

Angela waited, but her friend didn't finish her thought.

"You know what I'm saying," Brandie said.

Angela watched her mouth as she spoke, but she remained mute.

"Why you looking at me like that?" Brandie asked.

Angela shook her head. "I don't know. I think you're real pretty. Like, *exceptionally*. I wish my skin was like yours."

"You wouldn't say that if you grew up with it," Brandie said. "I've been called everything from midnight to jiggaboo, when I was growing up."

"I would never say anything like that about you. I think you're beautiful."

"*Okaaay*," Brandie replied. "And I'm also gay. So you can understand why this might be a little awkward; the way you're talking and looking at me."

"I'm sorry," Angela said. "I don't wanna make you feel weird."

"*Me?*" Brandie snickered. "I'm the one who's trying not to make *you* feel weird. I understand my situation, and I understand yours. And I'll always be respectful. But sometimes the way you look at me..."

Angela's heart thudded. She knew Brandie caught her staring a few times in the dorm. Angela was dying to know what was going through her friend's mind, but Brandie changed the subject.

"Never mind. You ready to go? The rain's only going to get worse."

Angela wished they could finish the conversation. She was close to divulging her biggest secret. She couldn't do it on her own, but if Brandie asked a few more poignant questions, Angela would've been honest with her. Instead her roommate stood and slipped on her jacket.

"You ready?"

Angela nodded. "Yes, I'm ready to go swimming."

"It won't be that bad," Brandie said with a chuckle.

But she was wrong about that.

≈ ≈ ≈ ≈ ≈ ≈

Brandie's umbrella was nice and sturdy, but the brutal winds turned it inside-out the second the heavy library doors swung closed behind them. Angela and Brandie held hands and screamed as they raced to their dorm. They were completely soaked when they got there. They laughed loudly when they reached the safety of the vestibule. They were still laughing when they got upstairs and began to strip off their rain-soaked clothes.

When they got down to their undies, Brandie called first dibs on the shower. Angela grabbed her Baby Phat robe and wrapped it around her shivering flesh. Brandie turned back to ask if she could borrow her roommates shampoo, and she caught Angela with one arm in her robe and both eyes clearly glued on Brandie's ass. There was no denying it. Angela's face flushed with heat, and Brandie's head tilted slowly to the side as she tried to make sense of her friend.

"I'm sorry," Angela said. Her wet hair hung in her face. She pulled her robe closed, but Brandie was still exposed in her bra and panties.

"I don't understand you," Brandie finally said. "Why do you keep looking at me like that?"

"I, I don't know," Angela said. Her heart was thumping again. Her eyes were wide and nearly fearful.

"Do you know how awkward this is for me?" Brandie asked. "I mean, I'm gay, and my roommate's straight, and I've been doing everything I can to keep things cool between us. If I was looking at you like that, you'd think I was coming on to you. So I have to be extra careful, because I am attracted to you. But you're not gay. I know you're not trying to give me any signals, but I feel like I'm getting them. I'm just, it's confusing."

"I'm sorry."

"Stop apologizing."

"I'm confused, too," Angela said. "I didn't know you were attracted to me."

"That's because I know how to keep my cool around straight girls," Brandie said.

"I'm attracted to you, too," Angela said. She spoke so softly. Her voice was barely audible over the raindrops spattering on their window.

"*But you're not gay,*" Brandie stressed. She sounded like she wished that weren't the case. Angela further confounded the situation by not responding.

Brandie frowned and took a step forward. Her expression softened. She had her hair pulled back in a ponytail. Her curly extensions were soaked and still dripping down her back. Her breasts were almost spilling out of her bra. They were so big and smooth. Angela wanted to bury her face in them.

"Angie, why won't you say you're not gay?"

Angela shrugged and shook her head vacantly. "I don't know."

"Are you gay?" Brandie dared to ask.

Angela continued to shake her head. She stared into Brandie's eyes, but her vision ran out of focus. Nervous goose bumps sprouted on her arms. Her heart was knocking.

Brandie approached her and looked pained when she said, "You know I like you. Why you doing this? Why you playing games?"

"I'm not," Angela said quickly. Her lips glistened from her cherry lip gloss. Her wet hair hung in her face.

Brandie nibbled her bottom lip. Her chest rose and fell. Angela became mesmerized by those chocolate mounds. She tried to make out Brandie's nipples through the thin fabric.

"Do you like me?" Brandie asked.

Angela nodded. Her eyes flicked from Brandie's face to her breasts and back again.

Brandie placed a hand on her shoulder. She barely touched her, but Angela felt a jolt of energy that rolled through her chest and settled right between her legs. It pulsated there, and Angela felt her kitty purr. She inhaled sharply. Her hand fell to her side, and her robe came open slightly.

Brandie's eyes rolled down Angela's frame. When she met her eyes again, she asked, "Can I kiss you?"

Angela half nodded. She blinked quickly and subconsciously moistened her lips. The room was very hot all of a sudden. Her whole body was on fire.

Brandie leaned in and closed her eyes, and the moment their lips touched something swelled in Angela's chest. There was a dull explosion; a sweet release that made her whole body shudder.

But as sweet as the kiss was, Angela was also hit with a powerful whirlwind of fear and uncertainty and other conflicting emotions. Her eyes flashed open. She took a step back, not believing what she had done. Was she drunk with passion, or was this really her? Was she gay, like Aunt Gayle? Could she do this, right now, or would she regret it afterwards and make the rest of her dorm time with Brandie very, very awkward?

As it turned out, things got very, very awkward anyway. Angela's hesitation was mortifying to Brandie. She didn't know if Angela mislead her or if she read the signs all the way wrong, but this was something Brandie had promised herself never to do.

Angela already dated a guy on campus. Regardless of how she might have looked at Brandie or responded to a question about her sexuality, Angela definitely was *not* gay. And Brandie wasn't a predator, running around trying to turn straight girls.

Brandie ran to the bathroom and was inconsolable for the rest of the night. Angela tried to smooth things over. Over the next few weeks, she told Brandie that she really did like her, she was just nervous because it was her first time. But it was no use. Brandie said they would remain friends and roommates *only*. She never should've crossed the line. Even if Angela was gay or bi-sexual, it was inappropriate for them to start a relationship while they were in the same dorm room.

The girls still hung out afterwards, but it was never the same. At the end of the semester, Brandie learned that her parents couldn't afford to put her in the dorm next year. She had to move back home. It was only a thirty minute commute, but it was enough to end Angela and Brandie's friendship their sophomore year. With no classes together, they only saw each other in passing. On those occasions, they did little more than wave and smile and then quickly try to push the memories of their freshman year from their minds.

≈ ≈ ≈ ≈ ≈ ≈ ≈

The former roommates didn't meet again until twelve years after their ill-fated kiss. Angela stopped at a Starbucks coffee shop on Friday afternoon to kill time while she waited for a client she was showing a home to. As she walked to the counter, Angela spotted Brandie seated at a table by herself. She stopped dead in her tracks. Her mouth and eyes widened at the same time. As she stood frozen, a flood of emotions rushed through her. Angela felt all of the fear and shame she felt on that violently rainy day. But her chest was also filled with the comfort and warmth and passion that came from her first kiss with another woman.

She was speechless as her mind sorted through these feelings. Brandie looked up from a newspaper she was reading, and her eyes widened as well.

"Angie? Angela Knight?"

Angela nodded as she approached her old friend. "Brandie Tucker. It's been a long time!"

Brandie rose from her seat and met Angela halfway. They embraced like long, lost sisters. It was a much different reaction than the casual nod they gave each other the last time they locked eyes at Texas Lutheran. Angela thought Brandie's fragrance was sweet and alluring. She inhaled slowly until the scent filled her lungs.

When they backed away, Brandie looked her up and down. Her eyes were bright, her smile sincere. "Wow, Angela, you look great!"

"You do, too," Angela said, and she meant it.

Brandie was just as gorgeous as she was in college. Her beautiful skin was without a blemish. Her full lips had a thin coat of fuchsia lipstick that matched her blouse. She wore a long skirt with black, knee high boots. Her facial features were more mature now, but it was Brandie's weight gain that was most surprising to Angela – but not in a bad way.

Brandie maintained a size six all the way through their senior year. Since graduation, she had developed some serious curves. Her hips spread, giving her an awesome waistline. Even through the skirt, Angela could see how thick Brandie's thighs were. And she had a sudden urge to get a peek at Brandie's backside. Angela admired women on TV all the time, but not since college had she been this attracted to a woman she met in person.

Angela viewed her bi-sexual desires as a little fire that sometimes got out of control, but for the most part smoldered quietly somewhere deep down in her soul. The last time it flared up like this, she and Brandie were alone in their dorm room, soaking wet. Angela began to wonder if she ran into her today because Brandie played a part in her destiny. Rather than a decade ago, she felt as if their one kiss happened just yesterday.

"What have you been up to?" Brandie asked. "What are you doing here?"

"I came here to wait on a client," Angela said. Both ladies were beaming. "Are you by yourself? Do you mind if I join you?"

"No, please," Brandie said. She waited for Angela to sit down before she returned to her seat.

They smiled and stared at each other for a few moments.

"So, what have you been up to since college?" Angela finally asked.

"I'm a teacher," Brandie said. "I work at Sunrise Elementary."

"I went to that school!"

"It's a great place," Brandie said. "I love it. I've been there for four years."

"That's awesome. I bet you're a great teacher."

"What about you?" Brandie asked. "What did Miss Angela end up doing with her life?" She took in the slacks and blouse Angela wore today. "Something successful, I see..."

"Not really," Angela replied. "I got a degree in business, but I work as a real estate agent."

"That's a good job," Brandie said.

"It's actually a lot better now. Three years ago we couldn't *give* a house away. Now things are almost back to normal."

"You've been doing it for a while?"

"Yeah, but I'm already thinking about branching out and doing my own thing. I just need to get my broker license."

"I'm surprised you haven't done it yet," Brandie said good-naturedly. "You've always been the type that likes to be in control."

"Really?" Angela said. "I don't remember that."

"You don't remember when you revamped study hall?" Brandie asked. "It was only our second day there, and you started demanding changes."

"Oh, that was because they didn't have enough tutors in there," Angela recalled. "And the room was way too noisy. It was better after they made those changes. Wasn't it?"

"Yes, it was better," Brandie said with a chuckle.

"Was it really?" Angela asked. "I didn't think I was bossy. Was I?"

"No," Brandie shook her head. She had her hair pulled back in a ponytail, drawing attention to her large eyes. "You weren't that bossy."

"I wasn't *that* bossy?"

"You know Angela always got her way," Brandie said. "Don't worry. It's a good thing."

"*Okay*," Angela said doubtfully. "I just wanted to make sure I didn't leave any bad impressions with anyone, with you…"

"No, of course not," Brandie replied. "You were my best friend during our freshman year. I don't think I would've passed algebra without you."

Angela smiled, but Brandie's comment was bittersweet. They were best friends during their freshman year, but after that they weren't, even though they both continued at the university until graduation.

"So what else has been going on with you?" Brandie asked. "Married? Any kids?"

Angela shook her head. "Nope."

"Really? Neither one?"

"Uh-uhn. What about you?" Angela blushed. What was she thinking?

But Brandie smiled. "No. I'm still gay."

"I'm sorry," Angela said. "I don't know why I asked that."

"It's natural," Brandie said. "You see an old friend, and you ask if they got married yet. It's natural. Nothing wrong with that."

Maybe not, but Angela knew that gay couples couldn't marry in Texas. Bringing it up might have been hurtful, if Brandie was in a serious relationship. Speaking of which...

"So, what are you doing today?" Angela asked. "You meeting somebody?"

"Yeah," Brandie said. "This guy I met on Craigslist. He's meeting me here to show me a laptop."

Remembering a few Craigslist murders last year, Angela's first thought was *DANGER*.

"You're meeting a stranger from Craigslist? Do you want me to stay with you until he gets here?"

"No, that's alright," Brandie said with a smirk. "That's why I told him to meet me here, somewhere public."

"These people aren't going to do anything if he comes in here and starts punching you," Angela said. "They might call the police, but they won't jump in and stop it."

Brandie laughed. "Why would he come in here and start punching me?"

"I don't know," Angela said. "People are crazy."

"I'm not that worried about it," Brandie said. "Anyway, what are you saying? You would jump in and defend me?"

"I would," Angela said sincerely.

"I appreciate that," Brandie said. "But I think I'll be alright. I got some pepper spray in my purse."

"Yeah, but..." Angela trailed off because her cellphone started to ring. She removed it from her purse and was a little chagrined to see her client's phone number. "Hold on a sec," she told Brandie. "Hello? Okay. I'll be there in three minutes."

She hung up and said, "Hey, I gotta go. My client is there already."

"Okay." She and Angela rose to their feet at the same time. "It was nice seeing you again."

"You should give me your number," Angela offered, "so I can check with you later. You know, to make sure you didn't have any trouble with this laptop guy."

Brandie frowned. Angela knew her pickup line was lame. If a guy told her the same thing, she'd think he was full of bull. But Angela never picked up a woman before (if that's what she was doing now), and she had to admit that she had no game.

Brandie's features soften, and she rattled off a number. Angela quickly punched the digits in her phone and stored it.

"Good luck with your client," Brandie said. "It was really nice seeing you again."

"Thanks," Angela said. "It was nice seeing you, too. I'll call you later."

≈ ≈ ≈ ≈ ≈ ≈

Angela's client was a jerk. He was a basketball player for the Dallas Mavericks. He was high profile, and she knew he was married. The whole city knew it. Angela also knew that the hoochie hanging on his arm, calling him *Daddy*, was not his wife. The handsome baller was no doubt securing a love nest for his mistress.

But business is business. The client wasn't picky, and his girlfriend was thrilled to get a house, any house, in return for her bedroom acrobatics. They were ready to close the deal in less than an hour.

Angela called Brandie later that day, before she went to meet Keshaun at the gym.

Brandie told her, "I made it home just fine, Angela. Thank you."

They chitchatted for a few minutes before Angela summoned the courage to say, "Do you think we could get together sometime, to catch up some more?"

After a noticeable pause, Brandie said, "Um, I guess so."

Angela didn't like the feeling of rejection that response gave her. She wanted to be open about why she wanted to see Brandie again, but she didn't want to say it over the phone. They made arrangements to meet for lunch the next day.

When she hung up, Angela decided that if her feelings for Brandie were serious, now would be a good time to confide in her best friend. She doubted that Keshaun would give her any objective advice, but Angela was dying to tell *somebody*.

CHAPTER THREE
THE DATE

For her date on Saturday (which probably wasn't a date from Brandie's perspective) Angela wore a white skirt with a sleeveless, grapefruit colored top. It was a warm, March afternoon, so she opted for open-toed sandals with two inch heels. Angela had butterflies in her stomach when she styled her hair and checked her makeup in her bathroom mirror. She was past the point of wondering if she was really going to partake in an *experience* with a woman.

The only question now was whether Brandie would be receptive, or if she was still resentful because of what happened in college. Maybe Brandie was already in a relationship. Angela wasn't interested in looking for someone else. She didn't want to date another female, if she couldn't have Brandie.

≈ ≈ ≈ ≈ ≈ ≈

She met her college roommate at the Pappadeaux seafood restaurant near the zoo district. Brandie wasn't there when Angela arrived. She entered the restaurant a few minutes later looking absolutely delectable in tight blue jeans and heels with a short-sleeved blouse that showed off quite a bit of the eye-catching cleavage Angela fell in love with years ago. The ladies hugged briefly before following the hostess to their table.

They made small talk through their appetizer and most of their entrée. Brandie wore her hair down this afternoon. Her makeup was flawless. Angela couldn't shake her nervousness as she stared at her old friend. She sensed Brandie might be a little uncomfortable as well.

"So, whatever happened to Keshaun?" Brandie asked after placing her fork on the table and dotting her lips with a cloth napkin. "Do y'all still keep in touch?"

"Yeah." Angela smiled. "I saw him yesterday at the gym."

"Still buddy-buddies, or are y'all living together by now?"

"We're just friends," Angela said. "After all these years."

"That's nice," Brandie replied. "Y'all had a lot of fun together."

Angela nodded. "We did."

Another awkward silence ensued. Angela saw Brandie check her watch, and her heart started to thud again. She took a deep breath and dried her moist palms on the napkin in her lap.

"I, um, there's a reason I wanted to see you today."

Brandie nodded slightly and gave her an encouraging smile. "What is it, Angela? You look nervous."

"I am. It's um..." She cleared her throat. "It's about what happened in, um, in college."

Brandie's eyes widened for a moment, and then she shook her head. "Angela please don't start apologizing for that again. It's over. No hard feelings. I told you that a hundred times. We–"

"I know," Angela said. "I don't want to apologize. Well, I do, but that's not what I wanted to talk to you about. But it does have something to do with, um, with that." *God.* She was rambling. Angela thought Brandie was starting to look at her like she was crazy.

"I still like you, and I wanted to know if you want to go out," Angela blurted. Her face flushed. Her eyes darted in embarrassment. When she finally met Brandie's gaze again, her friend was staring right at her. Of course she was. Brandie's lips were parted, but she didn't say anything, not for what felt like a long time.

"Okay, this is like, really embarrassing now," Angela muttered.

Brandie broke the tension with a wide smile. It was a sexy smile, or maybe Angela's mind was in the gutter.

"I was just struck with a strong sense of déjà vu," Brandie said.

"Me too," Angela managed.

"So after all these years, you still don't know what you want," Brandie said.

"I do know what I want," Angela countered.

"Have you been with a woman?"

Brandie kept her voice low, but Angela still looked around to make sure no one was listening to them before she shook her head.

"Then it is still the same," Brandie said. "I don't know why you picked me to have these revelations with, but if you've never been with a woman, then you're probably never going to be. Am I the only gay person you know? I'm sure there's *someone* in your life you can talk to about this stuff."

Angela was already apprehensive. Brandie's condescending tone made her feel even worse. She knew she deserved it, after what happened to them in college, but she didn't like to be talked down to.

"Yes there are people I can talk to about it," Angela said. "And I have talked to some of them. I'm not confused about what I want. Just because I haven't acted on it doesn't mean it's going away. I didn't ask you to come here to help me sort out my feelings. I asked you because I've always been attracted to you, for as long as I've known you. And when I ran into you yesterday, I felt like I had to take a chance."

"Take a chance on what?" Brandie asked.

Angela blushed again. "To see if you were seeing anyone, or whatever. I wanted to know if you still liked me." Angela closed her eyes briefly as she took a deep breath and let it out. There. It was out in the open. The worst Brandie could do at this point was reject her.

But Brandie smiled, and Angela half-smiled too.

"Angela, surely you'll understand if I have a hard time believing you're gay."

Angela nodded. "Yes, I understand. And I don't know if I'm fully gay. I still like men, but I also like women."

"You said the same thing in college."

"I know."

"And since then, you've only been with men... Right?"

"Yes," Angela said. "This is something I've been trying to sort out for years."

"But why me?" Brandie asked. "I think if you were going to act on your feelings, you would've done so by now."

"I don't know why I haven't acted on them," Angela said honestly. "But I'm positive I will at some point. Seeing you did, um, reignite some feelings I've had. You're the first woman I kissed. You're the only one. And I always thought we should've..." Angela felt the muscles between her legs clench, and she couldn't finish her sentence. When she looked up, Brandie was still smiling.

"Do you think I'm a fool?" Angela asked her.

"No."

"But you think I don't know what I'm talking about?"

"I used to feel the same as you," Brandie said. "*Many* years ago. I didn't know what I wanted, as far as men or women. But I made my decision in middle school. I haven't looked back since."

"Are you saying it's too late for me to make a decision?"

Brandie shook her head. "No."

"But you're saying you don't like me like that anymore?" Angela ventured.

Brandie licked her lips. Maybe on purpose, maybe not. "I still find you very attractive," she said.

Angela grinned, even though the whole room grew a few degrees warmer. "Are you seeing anyone?"

"No," Brandie replied. "But I want to hear more about why you think you're ready for this, if you want me to take you seriously."

Angela nodded. "Okay."

"Would you like something to drink?" Brandie asked as she summoned their waiter.

"Yes, very much so."

Brandie chuckled. "Margaritas or wine?"

"Margaritas."

"Could you bring us a couple of margaritas?" Brandie asked when their waiter approached. "Patron. And could we move to a booth, like that one over there?" Brandie pointed to a more secluded area of the restaurant.

"Yes, Ma'am," their waiter said. "That's not a problem. Right this way."

He waited while the women gathered their things.

≈ ≈ ≈ ≈ ≈ ≈ ≈

"I feel like there's something that's always been missing," Angela confided.

She leaned forward with her elbows on the table. Brandie sat across from her in the same position. They were very close. Both of their drinks were nearly empty. The alcohol in Angela's system emboldened her. She wasn't nervous at all as she revealed her deepest secrets. Brandie was a good listener. She only asked a few questions, otherwise letting Angela get everything off her chest.

Angela's admission that this was more than a *getting reacquainted* lunch changed the whole feel of the date. Brandie smiled a lot more, and she seemed to hang on every one of Angela's words. Angela thought Brandie was flirting with her; the way she'd laugh at all of her jokes and occasionally reach across the table to touch her hand. Angela, in return, was definitely flirting with Brandie. She'd look away coyly whenever Brandie narrowed her eyes or caught Angela staring at her cleavage or her beautiful lips. Brandie really was gorgeous. Angela thought that anyone who got this close to her (male or female) would quickly become as enamored as she was.

"The thing that's missing," Brandie said, "how sure are you that it's a woman?"

"I'm a hundred percent positive," Angela said.

"You're in your thirties," Brandie said. "Men have been pleasing you since the first time you had sex. If you're getting bored with them, maybe it's something they could do to spice things up."

"Why are you steadily trying to talk me out of it?" Angela asked.

Brandie smiled. "I'm not trying to talk you out of it. I just need to know that you're sure."

Angela smiled, too. "I already told you I was sure. Do you want me to prove it to you?"

Brandie's eyes widened for a moment before narrowing slightly. "That's, um…" She chuckled. "That's a very exciting proposition, Angela. But what you're asking me to do is pretty major. I hope you don't mind if I want to be extra cautious."

"What have I asked you to do?"

"You said you wanted me to be the first woman you dated."

Angela blushed. "Yeah, I did say that."

"I think that's a huge move for you as well," Brandie said. "I think you're beautiful, Angela. You're smart and funny. You're the kind of girl I would go for. But being someone's first… That's something I'm not interested in – unless I'm completely sure they're ready."

Angela nodded. It was exhilarating to hear that Brandie thought she was beautiful and she was her type. She also found it endearing that Brandie wasn't willing to jump into the situation until Angela satisfied all of her doubts. She had never met a man who asked, '*Are you sure? Are you sure you're sure?*' after she said she wanted to be with him.

"What I'm missing in my life is not a man," she said. "It isn't some new sexual position, and it's not a sex toy or anything like that. I like being with men, but I don't want to be with a man right now. I want to be with someone soft and *feminine*. I want to see a woman's breasts and nipples and panties. I want to feel a woman's lips on me. I want to hear and feel a woman's voice whispering in my ear.

"I want to feel all of these things while making love, and I don't need a dick or some man grunting on me all the time. I know that there's a lot more to what I currently know about life and love, and I'm not content anymore. This isn't just about sex. I want to experience a relationship with a woman in all aspects. I know this is a new chapter of my life, and I'm ready for it. I'm excited about it, and I hope you're willing to, to share this journey with me."

She reached across the table and took Brandie's hand in hers. Brandie stiffened for a moment before she held her back.

"What's wrong?" Angela asked. "Am I asking for too much?"

Brandie shook her head. "No, it's, it's fine. I'm, uh… *Whew*." She fanned herself with her free hand and chuckled nervously. She sighed. "No, it's not too much, Angela. It's a very exciting role, for me. It's actually really wonderful."

"Does that mean you'll do it?"

Brandie nodded and smiled. "Yes, Angie. I would love to go out with you. I promise I'll treat you like a lady."

Angela felt a great wave of euphoria wash over her. Her heart began to knock in her chest, but this time, rather than fear the unknown, Angela's blood ran hot in anticipation of what was to come.

≈ ≈ ≈ ≈ ≈ ≈

When they left the restaurant, the sun was still high in the sky. Brandie walked Angela to her car and lingered there, much like the men who had come before her had done after dates with them. When she approached for a hug, Angela was receptive. The feel of Brandie's arms wrapped around her made Angela grin like a much younger girl. But when Brandie leaned closer for a kiss, Angela couldn't help but turn away. Brandie let go of her, but she didn't look upset.

"I'm sorry," Angela said.

"Let me guess, you don't kiss on the first date."

Angela nodded. "Yeah. I know that's stupid." She found it hard to meet her friend's eyes.

"It's not stupid," Brandie said. "It's pretty cool. Says a lot about you."

Angela smiled nervously.

"*However*," Brandie went on, "I have to take our past into consideration. The last time I kissed you, you had such a strong reaction... It hurt my feelings, and I think it changed our friendship from that point on."

Angela nodded. Would they ever get past that incident in college?

"You're telling me that you're sure this time," Brandie continued. "I want to believe you. But I have to look after myself, too. I don't want to get hurt any more than you do."

Angela stared into her eyes. She saw that beyond Brandie's strength and beauty, there was also fear and vulnerability.

"So if we kissed, and you *didn't* freak out like last time," Brandie said. "That would go a long way in making me feel more comfortable about this, about our situation."

Angela thought that explanation was reasonable. Her eyes darted again as Brandie approached, but Angela didn't have time to see if anyone was watching before she closed her eyes and gave in to the experience.

The moment Brandie's lips came in contact with hers, Angela felt the pressure and anxiety in her chest loosen. It twisted in a whirlwind that swirled in her stomach and in her head. Brandie placed a hand on her waist. Angela felt a pulse of electricity in her touch. She couldn't help but gasp. Brandie moved closer still, until Angela felt her breasts press against her own.

Oh my God! I'm doing it! I'm kissing a girl! But that wasn't exactly true, because Angela hadn't done anything to reciprocate.

With her eyes still closed, she reached for Brandie and placed both hands on her hips. Gradually she kissed her back. Angela's hand moved slowly towards the small of Brandie's back as she sucked her bottom lip. Urged on by Angela's touch, Brandie stepped even closer, until there was but a sliver of space between their hips. Brandie's hands ran up Angela's sides and then came together at her spine.

Brandie's lips parted, and her tongue darted, tentatively. When Angela felt it, she opened her mouth and was ready when it appeared a second time. Their tongues met like midnight lovers and danced like mating serpents. The scent of Brandie's perfume was heavenly. Angela felt her arousal growing, low in her belly. She felt the muscles squeeze between her legs again.

She was backed into her car. Her hips pushed forward on their own accord. Brandie pushed back with more pressure, until Angela's butt pressed against the driver's door of her Tahoe. Angela had to spread her legs slightly to accommodate her. She sucked Brandie's tongue while Brandie's hands moved steadily upwards. Her left hand came to a rest behind Angela's neck. Her right hand gently cupped the side of Angela's breast.

This was more PDA than Angela would've allowed a man – any man – but she never felt as alive as she did in Brandie's arms. Plus this wasn't simply a first date kiss. It was confirmation for both Brandie and Angela. It meant her decision wasn't lofty. It was real, and their passion was real, and Angela wasn't going to run off like a confused, little girl when it was over.

After what felt like a full, blissful minute, Brandie backed way. She watched Angela who was heated and red about the face and chest but not regretful at all. Brandie reached to wipe a trace of lipstick that had smudged past Angela's lips. Angela watched her eyes. She had to fight a strong urge to take Brandie's thumb into her mouth and suck it.

"That was some kiss," Brandie finally said. "How you feeling?"

"I'm good," Angela said. She grinned sheepishly. "I liked it. A lot."

"No regrets?" Brandie asked.

"No," Angela said with a chuckle. "Not at all. I told you, I'm serious about this. It's not even up for debate anymore. This is who I am."

Brandie smiled, too. Angela saw that some of her lipstick was blended with her friends; creating a whole new shade of pink. For some reason, she found that awfully sexy.

"Okay," Brandie said. "I won't ask you about it anymore. I know you're not completely over men. I'm not happy about that, but I can accept you for who you are. I only ask that while you're seeing me, please let me know if you decide to date someone else. I only date one person at a time, and I only date girls who do the same."

"Me, too," Angela assured her. "You don't have to worry about that."

Brandie beamed. "Alright, Angie. I'm glad we're on the same page. I had a nice time this afternoon. I'll call you later." She leaned closer and kissed her again, briefly, before walking away.

Angela stood frozen with her smile stuck in place. Brandie looked good coming, but she looked damn good going, too! Angela couldn't believe she might one day get her hands on that plump booty! She laughed when she caught herself ogling.

Wow. I think I've become Keshaun.

That thought had her giggling all the way home.

My God this galactic wonder
Supreme physique. I long to plunder
To ravage – Ah, I've gone too far
Yet light is ebbing. In this dark
The shadows make me bold. Your toes
Are cold. I kiss each one. Behold
Each kiss is higher than the one
Before. Each kiss gets to the point
Your scent – exotic taste, it's just
Too much, to touch, it's such a rush
So plush your intersection is
This lust – this pleasure that you give
My will is yours. I yield. Just come
Here, let me show you, love. Just cum

CHAPTER FOUR
FIRST TIME

Over the next few weeks, Angela found that dating a female was different, but not totally dissimilar to dating a man. The courting was virtually identical. Brandie called Angela every day, and she sent her text messages sometimes, saying things like, "Morning cutie" around breakfast time and "Thinking bout cha" at lunch.

Angela always flirted back. By the third week she upped the ante by texting, "What color panties you got on?" at random times. One night Brandie took a pic of her flat stomach and low-rider jeans and sent it as a response. The top of her panties were visible in the photo, and Angela saw that they were teal. She stared at the picture for quite awhile, wondering what it would be like to twirl her tongue in Brandie's belly button.

One big difference between dating a woman and a man was the amount of care Angela took when she got ready for a date with Brandie. Angela knew what parts of her body she wanted to draw attention to – that was the same with both sexes. But for Brandie, Angela had to pay much more attention to her wardrobe.

A man would only notice that she had on sexy sandals. But a woman would pay attention to the brand name and check for scuffs and subconsciously decide if the sandals were a good choice for the outfit. Each time Angela went out with Brandie, she had to make sure her hair and makeup was flawless. Brandie was always a vision of perfection, so Angela knew she did the same thing.

≈ ≈ ≈ ≈ ≈ ≈ ≈

On Friday, March 22nd, Angela met Keshaun at the gym for their weekly cardio grind. Angela was eager to talk to someone about her recent progress, and Keshaun was more than eager to hear about it. He questioned Angela thoroughly while he helped with her pre-workout stretches.

"Have y'all kissed again?"

Angela blushed and grinned and then lowered her gaze as she reached for her right tennis shoe; stretching the muscles in her back and legs. Keshaun watched and waited while she switched to her left foot.

"Yes," Angela said finally. "We have."

"Where'd y'all go for your second date?"

"We went to the mall to get some shoes, and then we got some ice cream."

"That's a date?"

"I don't know. It's different. It felt like a date at the ice cream shop."

"She don't take you out to eat or to the movies?"

Keshaun reached for her hands. Angela took hold of his huge paws and held tightly while he bent at the waist and stretched towards her. They sat facing each other with their legs spread and the soles of their sneakers touching. Angela never tried to look between Keshaun's legs in this position, and she didn't know that he was quite the opposite. Every now and then Angela would have a slight camel toe that was visible through her tights. Keshaun noticed it when they started stretching today, and he'd been sneaking glances at it for the past ten minutes.

"We're going to the movies tomorrow night," Angela said.

"That's your third date, right?"

"Yup."

"That means you're about ready to give her some, huh?"

Angela gave him a look, but she was still smiling.

"What does that mean?"

"I don't know. I've been thinking about it," Angela confided.

"Thinking about sleeping with her?"

"Yes, Keshaun. Isn't that what we're talking about?"

"I just like to hear you say it."

"Why? Why you got to be such a perv?"

"I can't lie: This whole thing is amazing to me," Keshaun explained. "I be thinking about y'all sometimes. I wonder what y'all doing, what y'all talking about. I'd pay you to wear a wire for me. I don't even need a video. I just want to hear one of your conversations."

Angela laughed.

"What's it like when you kiss her?" Keshaun asked.

"It's different," Angela said. "Her touch is different, than a man. Her smell is different. Her skin is softer. Everything is just, I don't know, more *feminine*."

"I *love* the way women feel," Keshaun mused. "I love their perfume, their hair, their breasts. They're so soft."

"Yes," Angela sighed. "Exactly."

"But you're not gonna get any dick," Keshaun said. "At some point all of that kissing and touching and stuff is gonna get old, and you'll want some hard dick – rammed all up in you!"

He laughed.

After covering her face in shame, Angela laughed, too.

"Tell me I ain't right," Keshaun said. "I know you gon' want some penetration – something longer and fatter than a finger."

"Shut up, boy. You so stupid."

"Am I wrong?"

"No, but you don't know anything about a woman pleasing another woman."

"Whatever. You don't either."

Angela chuckled. "I know more than you do."

"Tell me, then."

"Keshaun, there's all kinds of lesbians. Some want to be with a pretty, fashion model-type. Some want to be with a stud."

"What's a stud? Like a bull dyke? The ones who be cutting their hair and dressing like a man?"

"I don't think they like to be called *bull dykes*. But yeah, some women like that type."

"What that got to do with penetration?"

"I don't know, Keshaun. I never had sex with a woman. But from what I've heard, straight women like different kinds of sex, and lesbians do, too. Some only want the fingers and tongue. Some do like penetration, I think. Those are the ones who might get their partner to wear a strap-on."

Keshaun grinned. "The ones who like strap-ons, why don't they just get with a man? They could get the real thing."

"I don't know, Keshaun. I'm just as curious as you. I don't think a true lesbian wants the real thing," Angela said. "Some of them would throw up if they saw a penis squirting shit out of it."

Keshaun laughed again. "Is that the kind of lesbian Brandie is?"

"I have no idea," Angela said. "I never asked her. But I know she's not bi-sexual. She said she's never been with a man."

"How she know she don't like it, if she never tried it?"

"Keshaun, I'm not about to discuss someone else's sexual preferences with you. You said you knew she was gay in college. You should've asked her about it yourself, if you're so interested."

"Okay, well what about you?" he said. "When you sleep with Brandie, are you gonna ask her to use a dildo, or a strap-on? 'Cause I know *you* like penetration."

Angela couldn't deny that. Even if she tried, her grin would've given her away.

"Who said we're going to sleep together?"

Keshaun smacked his lips. "Come on, Angie. Ain't that the whole point? You wanted to see what sex would be like with a woman, right?"

"No, Keshaun. I want to have a *relationship* with Brandie – not just sex with some random woman."

"But you are going to sleep with her, right? You said she was fine."

"I would very much like to sleep with her," Angela admitted.

"You want me to give you some tips?" Keshaun asked. "'Cause you know I know how to get them panties off."

"Yeah right. Like you got game."

"I do got game."

"You just ask your girlfriends if you can suck on their clitoris," Angela said.

"Yup. Works every time. Have you told Brandie you want to suck on her clitoris?"

Angela blushed. "No, I haven't."

"Do you want to?"

"I've been thinking about it, a lot," Angela admitted.

"Damn," Keshaun said dreamily. "Do you promise to tell me about it?"

"Keshaun, just stop."

"I'll do anything," he said. "I'll even stop staring at your camel toe."

They were done with their stretching, so Keshaun didn't care when Angela rolled her eyes at him and stood abruptly. She pulled her tee-shirt down before she turned away, so he wouldn't stare at her ass when she walked off.

"You're nasty!"

Her tee shirt wasn't that long today, so Keshaun still got a good look at her assets.

Damn, he muttered to himself. He wanted Angela to be happy, but deep down he couldn't bear to lose her to the other team. If he could make love to her *one more time*, he'd worship her body like a temple. He'd lick her kitty until she was overcome with passion. And just when she convinced herself that she couldn't possibly cum again, he'd produce his sword. He'd fill her so completely and deeply, Angela would know that no other man *or woman* could ever satisfy her so fully.

All he needed was one night.

≈ ≈ ≈ ≈ ≈ ≈ ≈

The following evening Angela took Brandie to see the new Will Smith movie. Angela always found darkened theaters romantic, when she went with her boyfriends. It was still romantic with Brandie, but Angela soon realized she hadn't reached a level of comfort with her burgeoning bi-sexuality.

She didn't mind when Brandie reached to hold her hand midway through the flick, but Angela felt self-conscious when Brandie leaned closer and kissed the sensitive spot under her ear. There was a family of four sitting to the left of them, three spots down. Angela couldn't bring herself to make out with a girl while an eight year old boy munched popcorn six feet away. She bent her head towards her shoulder, effectively forcing Brandie's lips away from her neck. A few minutes later, when Brandie tried to play vampire again, Angela pulled the same maneuver. This time she giggled and said, "Stop," hoping to keep things lighthearted.

But Brandie let go of her hand and kept her attention on the big screen for the rest of the movie. She was noticeably withdrawn when they left the theater. When Angela took her home, Brandie said, "Thanks. See you later," and hopped out of the car without offering a goodnight hug or kiss. Angela got out, too, and she caught up with Brandie on her doorstep.

"Wait. Are you mad at me?"

"I'm just tired," Brandie said. She was clearly irritated. "I really don't have time to figure out what's going on with you or where your head's at. I been doing just fine, Angie. This is why I don't date virgins."

Angela almost told her she was far from a virgin, but she realized Brandie was right.

"I'm sorry," she said. "There was a boy watching us in the movies. I didn't–"

"He wasn't watching us," Brandie said. "Even if he was, you wouldn't have gave a damn if you were with a man. I know I'm not all that, but I don't make a habit of trying to kiss girls who are steadily rejecting me. I have my own standards. But more important than that, I have feelings, too."

Brandie's eyes glistened. Angela's heart bled for her. She approached and wrapped her arms around her small waist. Brandie stiffened. She was taller, so Angela had to look up to kiss her. Brandie didn't kiss her back, not right away. She didn't reciprocate until Angela caressed her back and probed her mouth with her tongue.

A moment later the soft, wet sounds of their kiss filled the night as their fingers skated across each other's bodies. Brandie's hands were like heat pads, igniting little fires on every piece of flesh she touched. Angela moaned when she had Brandie's plump booty in both hands. It felt absolutely wonderful. She had been with men who had nice, round asses, but they were usually more muscular. Brandie's booty was so soft, Angela could use it as a pillow.

"Your ass feels so good," she breathed between kisses.

Brandie's hands slipped to Angela's cheeks, and she said, "I think yours feels much better."

Angela let go of her ass so she could embrace her fully. There was a fire raging in her belly and a dampness in her panties. She was beyond ready, but Brandie didn't ask her to come inside.

"I'm sorry about earlier," Angela said. Her lips brushed Brandie's jugular as she spoke. She kissed her neck and then suckled the same spot. "Forgive me?"

"Yes," Brandie said.

Angela felt Brandie's chest rise and fall against her own. She thought Brandie was ready, too, but she still didn't get an invite. It was driving Angela crazy. If she came on to a man like this, he would've thrown her over his shoulder and kidnapped her for the next few hours.

"But I'm no one's secret," Brandie said. "Or their side-piece, or whatever."

"I know," Angela said. "I'm sorry. I won't do that again."

But even as she spoke, Angela knew that she couldn't hug and kiss Brandie like this if they were in a public setting. She hoped she'd have time to get over this hump before Brandie got frisky one day and called her bluff.

≈ ≈ ≈ ≈ ≈ ≈

On Wednesday the following week, Angela had a vivid daydream about Brandie while prepping a property for an open house. She stopped for a moment to send her girlfriend a text message: "On the west side, showing a house. Just thought about you, on this bearskin rug"

Brandie replied to her a few minutes later, also via text. "Sounds nice. Is it soft?"

"Not as soft as your booty," Angela responded.

A moment later Angela's cellphone vibrated in her pocket. Her whole body grew warm when she read the message: "You wouldn't know what to do with it"

Angela quickly typed her response: "You the one who wouldn't let me in your house"

Brandie said, "I know. Cause you ain't ready"

Angela typed quickly with her thumbs, "Do I have to beg?"

Brandie said, "Yes"

On Angela's side of town someone rang the doorbell at her open house. Before she answered, she took a page from The Book of Keshaun for her next message: "May I please suck your clitoris?"

Angela was busy entertaining perspective buyers for the next hour. A mischievous grin spread across her face when she had time to check her phone again.

Brandie said, "I'll be home at 5. Cum at 6"

Angela wiped the sweat from her brow and typed, "Did you spell that wrong?"

Brandie's response came within seconds. "Nope"

≈≈≈≈≈≈

Angela knocked on her door at 4:52. Brandie answered wearing a blood red robe. It was satin. It blended smoothly with the crimson tones in her dark skin. Her hair was perfect. It flowed from her scalp in soft curls, concealing most of her left eye. She was barefoot. Her toenail polish matched her robe. Her feet sank into her soft carpet. Angela had an immediate urge to take her shoes off, too. She wanted to take Brandie's robe off. She inhaled slowly and audibly.

Brandie looked back at a wall clock mounted above her television and said, "You're early."

"I've been waiting in my car for five minutes," Angela admitted. "Got impatient."

Brandie smiled. Her lips were plump. Angela blushed. "Come in."

Angela had never been inside her house. Brandie lived a modest lifestyle, but she tended to splurge on clothing and electronics. Her entertainment center was a work of art. The lighting in the front room was dim.

"Have a seat," Brandie told her as she continued walking towards the kitchen.

Angela sat nervously on the sofa and looked around the room. A mellow Luther Vandross tune oozed from the stereo like honey. He sang about a mistake that cost him his woman and how he was not meant to live alone. His voice gave Angela chills. She saw a framed photograph from the Alvin Ailey Dance Theater on the opposite wall. The powerful, black dancers were in the midst of leaping. They were beautiful, like Brandie. Angela wondered if Brandie was a dancer; if that was why she stood with such poise and always exuded confidence.

Brandie returned with a bottle of wine in one hand and two half-full glasses in the other. She gave a glass to Angela before placing the bottle on a coaster that was already on the table. She sat down, and Angela shuddered when their knees brushed.

71

Brandie narrowed her eyes slightly and smiled. Angela took a sip of her wine and giggled.

Brandie asked her, "Have you eaten?"

Angela nodded. "I had a late lunch."

"Are you hungry?" Brandie asked. "You shouldn't drink on an empty stomach."

"No, I'm fine," Angela assured her. She took another sip of her drink and then a hefty swallow. She didn't realize she was parched. She cleared her throat and took another drink. Her glass was empty when she brought it away from her lips. Brandie raised an eyebrow.

"Sorry, I was thirsty," Angela said.

"You want some water?"

"No. Could I have some more wine, please?"

Brandie chuckled, and then she quickly downed her own drink. "Alright, if that's how we're rolling."

She poured another round for both of them. The alcohol in Angela's system was already helping to settle her nerves, so she took her time with this one.

"I'm nervous, too," Brandie said.

Angela didn't believe that. "Why?"

"Because you're a virgin," Brandie said. "That's a lot of pressure." She smiled.

Angela smiled, too.

"I know you're curious about being with a woman," Brandie went on, "and eager..."

She looked into Angela's eyes, and Angela looked down at her glass.

"But I have to ask you one more time: Are you sure you're ready?" Brandie said. "I don't want to be simply *your first time*. When I make love to a woman, I do it because she's the woman I want to be with."

"I want to be with you, too," Angela said. And she meant it. She never slept with anyone just for the sex. She was thrilled about being in a relationship with Brandie, and she knew the lovemaking would deepen their bond.

Brandie reached and brushed the hairs away from Angela's face. She leaned forward and kissed her softly. She suckled Angela's bottom lip and pulled it slightly with her teeth. The contact was brief, but Angela felt the impact like a kick to the chest. A tingling heat radiated down her legs, to her toes and then back up again. It came to a rest around her clitoris and began to throb pleasantly.

Brandie backed away and drank the rest of her wine. She placed the glass on the coffee table and slowly rose to her feet. She walked away without a word. Angela was hesitant to follow, but Brandie removed her robe just as she disappeared down the hallway. Angela's eyes widened. She didn't have time to see if Brandie had anything on beneath the robe. Angela stared at the discarded garment for a few seconds and then quickly finished her second drink. She placed the wineglass on the table and stood uneasily.

The slight friction her thighs created as she followed was tantalizing. Angela's heart thundered. She took a deep breath and tried to calm herself when she reached the hallway. Brandie was nowhere in sight, but there was an open bedroom door ahead on the left. Angela's heels sank in the plush carpet as she moved in that direction.

≈ ≈ ≈ ≈ ≈ ≈

The lights were off in Brandie's bedroom, but the sun hadn't set yet, so there was adequate lighting. Brandie stood before a king-sized bed wearing only a bra and panties. There was a lot to take in. Angela's senses were quickly overloaded. In her peripheral vision, she saw that Brandie's comforter was black and maroon colored, which matched the window curtains exactly. She saw that there were scented candles burning on two different dressers. Angela recognized the scent as lavender and chamomile. She still heard Luther playing in the living room. It wasn't the same song as before, so Angela knew it had to be one of his greatest hits albums.

But all of this was picked up in little pieces that didn't come together until later. Angela's immediate attention was drawn to the magnificent creature who stood no more than five feet away. Angela didn't mean to ogle, but Brandie's body was unreal. Her natural breasts swelled from the top of her bra, creating smooth hills of dark chocolate cleavage. Her waistline was small. Her hips protruded from her body at pleasing angles, giving her a natural hourglass figure.

Brandie's lingerie was royal blue. Angela couldn't fathom how the tiny bra maintained its hold on her breasts. As her eyes rolled lower, Angela marveled at how smooth Brandie's skin was. Her panty line was very low, and there was no visible pubic hair. Angela inhaled sharply as she stared between Brandie's legs. She could *almost* make out the contours of Brandie's kitty through the panties. She ached to touch it. She wanted to slide the panties to the side and slip a finger inside her hot moistness. She wanted to taste it. She still couldn't believe she was this close to making her dream a reality.

"Do you like my body?" Brandie asked.

Angela couldn't answer right away. She'd been with men who had awesome physiques, but no one ever asked her that question before. It was obvious she was enthralled. She nodded vacantly and stiffened when Brandie approached her.

"I like your body, too," Brandie said. "But it's really hard to tell right now..." She reached for Angela's chest and began to unbutton her blouse.

Angela stared dreamily into her eyes. Both arms hung limply by her sides.

Brandie asked, "Are you okay."

Angela nodded. She was more than okay. The two glasses of wine made her insides warm. She felt very relaxed. "I feel good."

Brandie's hands felt soft on Angela's chest and belly. When she unfastened the last button, she pulled the blouse off Angela's shoulders. Angela shook free of the button-down, and it fell to the floor behind her. Brandie put both arms around her waist. She traced two fiery fingers down Angela's spine, coming to a stop at the top of her skirt. She found the zipper and pulled it down slowly.

Angela stepped forward when the skirt fell around her ankles. She kissed Brandie again, and their tongues began their sultry dance. Brandie's taste was exotic. With her hands on Angela's hips, she turned them around, until Angela's back was to the bed. Brandie pressed into her. Angela took two steps back and she felt the mattress against her upper thighs. Brandie pushed further still. Their hips came together, and Angela felt the heat radiating from Brandie's love box.

She gasped. Brandie pushed her tongue deeper. She explored Angela's mouth while her fingers made their way to the back of her bra. She undid the clasp expertly and backed away just long enough to pull the bra completely off. Angela had goose bumps around her areola. Brandie stared at them for a moment, her mouth salivating. Her hands returned to Angela's hips, and she gently slid her panties down her long legs. Brandie bent and then squatted as she pulled the panties past Angela's knees and shins and finally around her ankles.

Before she stood, Brandie buried her face in Angela's nookie. The move was unexpected. Angela couldn't stop a startled moan from escaping her. Brandie inhaled her scents and kissed her labia before she rose to full height. When they were face to face again, she saw that Angela's breathing was slightly labored. Her chest rose and fell, pushing her boobs forward like an offering. Brandie accepted. She cupped both breasts and kissed them one at a time. Angela watched her tongue flick slowly, up and down and in a circular motion around her nipple. Within seconds it was hard and rigid.

"Ohhh."

Angela's whole body shuddered. Brandie moved to the opposite breast and brought her other nipple to a similar state of arousal. She then swallowed it whole, sucking and licking simultaneously. Angela felt a levee overflow in her kitty, and then she felt Brandie's hand there!

"Ah!"

Brandie left her breasts so that she could watch Angela's eyes. She rubbed her wet center with two fingers and gradually slid one of them between her labia. Angela was beyond moist. Brandie's bottom lip disappeared inside her own mouth. Angela watched her nostrils flare slightly.

"Damn, Angie," Brandie whispered. "You feel so good." She withdrew her fingers and brought them to her face. "You so wet," she said. She ran her fingers across her upper lip and slipped the longest into her mouth.

Angela's eyes widened as she watched her. She couldn't have been more aroused.

"Lay down," Brandie told her.

Angela sat on the bed and then scooted to the center. Brandie reached to undo her own bra before she followed. Angela wanted to be obedient, but once those melons were free, she had to have them in her mouth. She sat up and returned to the edge of the bed. Brandie had slipped her panties off by then. Angela saw that she was shaved, almost completely bare. She spread her legs, and Brandie quickly filled the space. Angela reached greedily for her breasts. The first touch was exhilarating. The first lick was 34 years in the making. But Angela didn't take a moment to consider how monumental this act was or how far she'd strayed off the path of "normalcy."

At that second she was a child at a chocolate factory, and all that mattered was her feast. Brandie's areolas were chocolate jelly rings. Her nipples were warm Raisinets. Angela didn't realize how ravished she was until she nibbled hard enough to make Brandie cry out.

"Uh!"

"I'm sorry." Embarrassed, Angela pulled away.

"No, do it again," Brandie urged. She reached and placed a hand behind Angela's neck when she didn't comply right away.

Angela was eager for more, but she was a lot gentler this time. Brandie's hand moved to the back of her head. She grabbed a fistful of hair.

"No, bite it," she commanded. "Bite it again."

Angela closed her mouth around her nipple and gently squeezed with her top and bottom teeth. She sucked and slowly increased pressure, but it wasn't enough. Brandie gripped her hair tighter and forced her face closer. Angela bit down with a little more force, and Brandie threw her head back and cried out in pleasure. Angela was startled. Brandie pushed her shoulders back and pulled Angela's legs up as they fell onto the bed.

Angela had been in this position before. She never considered a woman mounting her like this, and she didn't think anything would come of it. But then she felt Brandie's hot slit directly on hers. They were both wet to the point of leaking. Brandie pushed her further onto the bed with little assistance. With Angela's legs in the air, Brandie began to grind her hips, much like a man would. Angela stared up at her in awe. She felt Brandie's labia rubbing against her own. The friction was unexpectedly stimulating. Even more startling was how Brandie managed to brush her clitoris with each thrust.

Oh my God.

Angela's blood raced through her veins. She didn't know how this was possible. She wanted to crane her neck to see exactly what was going on down there. With no penetration, Brandie had her kitty purring. Angela dry-humped with boys when she was young, but Brandie's slow grind was something totally different. She obviously liked to dominate, and Angela was an attentive pupil. The sounds of their sex was foreign and delightful, but Angela could barely hear it over her moans of ecstasy and the blood rushing past her ears. She closed her eyes, and they rolled to the back of her head. She began to pump her hips upwards, ensuring that Brandie's clitoris continued to stimulate hers.

"Don't cum," Brandie whispered. She lowered her head and sucked Angela's upper lip.

"I can't, I can't..." Angela spoke into her open mouth. "I can't help it. Oh God. *Oh, oh God.*"

"Don't you want to cum in my mouth?" Brandie breathed.

"I can't... Oh shit. I can't stop."

Brandie disappeared, just as a pleasant tidal wave originated in Angela's chest and began to roll down her stomach. Her clitoris pulsated. Her vaginal walls contracted. Brandie's face reappeared between Angela's legs just as the wave of ecstasy made it past her belly button. Angela felt warm breath on her labia, and then she felt the softest, longest and hottest tongue lick her from bottom to top. Brandie wrapped her lips around her throbbing clitoris a split second before a powerful convulsion wracked Angela's entire body.

"Oh, oh, oh!"

Her orgasm was so powerful, she lost complete control of her legs. The muscles flexed randomly, pushing her ass off the bed. Brandie grabbed hold of her hips and continued to suck and lick her clitoris expertly. She didn't mind when Angela reached down and grabbed hold of her head with both hands. She didn't complain as Angela rode her orgasm and Brandie's face for nearly a minute until the convulsions subsided. Behind her closed eyelids, Angela saw pink and gray specs of light. She saw Brandie's face between her legs, but only from the nose up. That image would be stored in her memory bank for eternity. No one forgets their first.

She heard Brandie chuckling.

Angela smiled without opening her eyes. "Wh, what's so funny?"

"I barely touched you," Brandie said. Her face was still between her legs. Angela felt her breath on her thighs and ass.

"I know," Angela said. She slowly blew out a sigh.

"Can you stay the night?" Brandie asked. She kissed her labia softly.

Angela moaned. Her legs trembled, still in the throes of an awesome aftershock. "Yes," she said.

"I want to show you some things," Brandie said. She licked her again. "I love the way you taste. I could eat you for an hour." She licked her again.

81

Angela felt another eruption brewing. Her eyes fluttered open, and it was a struggle to sit up on her elbows. She felt completely drained. She looked down and locked eyes with Brandie. It was strange; seeing a woman's face there. But it was a good thing. Very nice.

"I want to taste you, too," Angela said. "I want you to teach me."

Brandie winked at her. "But of course. I am a teacher, after all." She smiled at her own joke and then went after the juices that were leaking from Angela's kitty. "Waste not, want not," she whispered.

CHAPTER FIVE
FOR A LIMITED TIME

The writing was on the walls. It had always been there. Angela knew that she was guilty of ignoring the signs. Even worse, she wondered if she blatantly turned a blind eye, so that she could get what she wanted. She didn't think that was the case, but after the shit hit the fan, she had to do some serious soul searching to determine if she really was the person Brandie painted her out to be.

The first red flag came on Thursday, the day after they made love. Angela was in a great mood at work. She felt refreshed and energized. A few of her coworkers noticed her glow, but they didn't comment on it until Angela returned from showing a house at noon.

"Hey," Katy said. She was a tall blonde with dark red lipstick that didn't look well against her pasty skin. She left her desk and sidled up to Angela. Katy's grin was big and dopey.

"What?" Angela asked her.

"You got a gift!" Katy announced.

Angela's body went numb when she rounded the corner and saw a beautiful vase on her desk. It was filled with blood red roses. Angela was aware that her reaction was the exact opposite of what her coworker expected, so she managed a weak smile.

"Wow."

"They're from *B*," Katy said. "Sorry, we already read the card. So, who's this B? A secret admirer? A new boyfriend?"

Angela used to think it was cute how Katy lived vicariously through her sometimes. Today she was irritated. How dare they violate her privacy like that? If the card wasn't addressed to *Katy*, then the bitch had no business reading it!

But that was wrong. Angela never had a problem basking in the attention and jealousy whenever one of her boyfriends had chocolates or flowers delivered to her workplace. The only difference now was *B* wasn't a boy.

"It's a new guy I met," Angela said. Her face flushed. She felt beads of sweat forming on her forehead.

"You must've made quite an impression, if he's sending flowers already!"

"What does he look like?"

Angela turned, surprised to see two more ladies hovering around her.

"Is he tall, dark and handsome?" Tisha asked.

"Of course he is," Gloria said. "All of Angela's boyfriends are tall, dark and handsome!"

"You don't date white guys?" Katy asked.

Angela shook her head absently and then nodded. "Um, I mean yeah, I have..."

"Why the mystery?" Gloria asked. "What's the B for? Brandon?"

"Or *Bruno*?" Katy guessed.

"*Bruno*?" Gloria frowned. "That's a dog's name!"

"Really? I like Bruno," Katy said.

"It's probably *Byron*!" Tisha said, and they all laughed.

"No, it's *Brandie*!" Angela spat. "These flowers are from a girl that I'm dating and falling in love with. That's right, a *girl*! And we already had sex, so I guess that makes me gay or bi-sexual or whatever kind of freak you think I am. So now what? What do you got to say about these fucking flowers now?"

But of course Angela didn't say any of that. She just smiled and pretended to be thrilled by the roses and the mysterious *B* who sent them.

≈ ≈ ≈ ≈ ≈ ≈

The second red flag didn't seem like one at the time. Two days after the flower delivery, Angela took Brandie to the movies – mostly to make up for upsetting her the last time they caught a flick.

The theater was mostly empty that night, and Angela didn't have a problem with any of the affection Brandie offered in the darkness. They left the movie in good spirits. Angela didn't realize they were still holding hands until they got outside. There was a new crowd of people lined up at the ticket booth. Among the crowd were three black men who immediately zeroed in on the two best looking females they'd seen all night.

Angela pulled her hand from Brandie's grip with little thought about what she was doing. She realized her mistake when Brandie turned to her with a confused look in her eyes. Brandie's expression became hurt and then angry when she saw the men that caused Angela's reaction.

But Brandie never said anything to indicate she was upset about the hand-holding incident. When Angela took her home, Brandie invited her inside for a night cap that quickly rolled into heavy petting. She didn't spend the night that day, but Angela definitely felt loved and forgiven when she left Brandie's house a few minutes after midnight.

≈ ≈ ≈ ≈ ≈ ≈ ≈

Angela's third and final mistake occurred on Wednesday, April 3rd, exactly one week after she and Brandie explored one another's bodies for the first time. Angela had a two-hour gap in her schedule, so she drove to Brandie's school and picked her up for a quick lunch. Brandie surprised her by suggesting McDonalds for their destination.

"McDonalds?"

"I only have forty-five minutes," Brandie said. "I don't have time to relax and wait for some stupid waitress."

"Okay," Angela said. "Mickey D's it is."

Angela hadn't been to the restaurant in some time. When they got there, she was excited to see that the McRib was back on the menu. Brandie ordered a Cobb salad and shook her head at Angela when they took a seat on one of the brightly-colored benches.

"What?" Angela said.

"You know the McRib is seasonal because of black folks..."

Angela laughed. "That's not true!"

"Yes it is," Brandie said. "Black people go crazy over those damned things. When they start hanging out at McDonalds too much, scaring all of the good white folks, they'll take it off the menu, until you niggas forget about it again. That's why they say: *For a limited time only, bitches!*"

"You are so full of it!"

Brandie laughed, too. "I bet I'm right, though. Why else would it come and go so much?"

"Because they're too expensive to make," Angela guessed. "When pork prices are up, there's no McRib. When they go down again, it comes back."

"If you think there's any real pork in that sandwich, you really are crazy!" Brandie joked.

They laughed, and then Brandie said, "Oh, I've been meaning to ask you something. My brother's play debuts this weekend. Can you come with me? It's Saturday night. Everybody's gonna be there. We're trying to pack the house for him."

Angela knew that Brandie had a brother who was trying to make it as a director/author. Angela expressed interest in seeing one of his plays a few weeks ago but didn't know if she was ready for the family affair Brandie was describing.

"Everybody, like who?" she asked.

"What you mean?"

"Who's gonna be there?" Angela asked. "You mean, like, your whole family?"

Brandie's beautiful eyes narrowed. "What difference does it make who's there?"

"I just..." Angela's pulse began to race. She knew this conversation wouldn't end well. "You, um, you make it sound like your whole family is gonna be there..."

"And?" Brandie said. "What about it?"

She was ready to go off, big time. Angela knew she could smooth things over by simply saying she'd attend the play, but she wasn't going to be bullied into such a big decision.

"Brandie, I don't think I'm ready to meet your family." She thought that sounded perfectly reasonable, but it didn't stop the tidal wave of anger and frustration that had been building up in her girlfriend's heart and soul for weeks.

"Bullshit." Brandie's sneer was hard enough to cut glass.

The last time Angela saw that much anger directed at her, she was in high school, and a girl named Tomeka Mann had both fists full of Angela's hair as they rolled around the gym floor in what felt like a fight to the death.

Angela swallowed hard. "We've only been going out for a month."

"Then why you sleep with me?" Brandie growled. "You didn't say that shit when you was trying to get what you wanted."

Angela looked around uncomfortably. Her eyes were wide, her mouth ajar. "Why are you raising your voice? And why are you so mad?"

"Because I fucked around and did something I knew I shouldn't have!" Brandie said. She tossed her fork into her salad and then sent the whole container crashing to the floor with a quick swipe of her beautifully manicured hand. Angela flinched, initially thinking Brandie was taking a swing at her.

The restaurant was packed, but thankfully it was after one, and the high school students who usually dined there at noon were all gone. There were still a few grown folks who flocked to the argument like moths to a flame. Angela couldn't have been more embarrassed. She buried her face in her hands and muttered, "Oh my God."

"You embarrassed?" Brandie shouted as she rose to her feet. "Am I embarrassing you, Angela? How do you think I felt when you pushed me away at the movies that time? How do you think I felt the other day when you snatched your hand away from me, like I got leprosy or something? How do you think that made me feel?!"

Angela looked up and saw tears in Brandie's eyes. She was truly regretful about everything she'd done to hurt her, but Angela didn't think she deserved this.

"Please stop."

"I am stopping," Brandie said. "I'm done! I don't got shit else to say!" She snatched up her purse and threatened the gawkers who had formed a wall of bodies around them. "*Get the hell out my way!*"

Angela looked at all of the grinning faces around her. She knew she could never show her face in that McDonalds again. She grabbed he purse and followed Brandie out.

"Brandie, wait."

By the time Angela got outside, Brandie was halfway across the main thoroughfare. She stood on the median with her back turned, waiting for a break in traffic on the other side. Angela couldn't believe it. It was a six lane street. And today's lunch hour looked like rush hour.

"Brandie!"

Her friend didn't turn around. Brandie found her chance to cross the street and took it. She didn't even run. She strutted across the pavement like a model on a catwalk.

Dammit!

Angela took off her heels and raced across the first three lanes. The asphalt was hot, and she stepped on a few sharp pebbles that made her wince. Angela had the light, so she didn't pause at the median. When she got to the other side of the road, she hobbled to Brandie with her shoes in one hand and her purse in the other. Her hair was out of place, her breathing nearly ragged.

"*Why are you running*?!" she bellowed.

Brandie spun on her. Thick tears snaked down her cheeks. "*Why are you chasing me*?!" she yelled back.

"What did you do that for?" Angela cried. "I didn't deserve that!"

"Neither did I!" Brandie countered. "I don't deserve any of your shit!"

"I was just saying I wasn't ready," Angela reasoned. "I didn't say I wouldn't go."

"But you said you *were* ready," Brandie snapped. "Before we even got into this, I told you; *you're not ready*, and you said you were! You argued me down."

"I said I was ready to be with you. I didn't say I was ready to meet your family."

91

"Or hold my hand in public," Brandie said. "Or kiss me in public."

"But, but why can't you give me a little time?" Angela said. "You know this is all new to me." Her features were twisted in pain. Brandie's were, too.

"Because I've done this before," Brandie said. "You think you're the first girl in the world to ask for some fucking *time*? What am I supposed to do during this *time*? Huh? Be your little secret?"

"No, I didn't say that."

"How many times do you think I gave *time* to some bitch who never came out of the closet?"

"I'm not like them."

"You're *just* like them!" Brandie shouted. "You wanted to know what sex would be like with a woman, and you got what you wanted. That's all you wanted, so why the hell are you following me?"

"That's not true."

"Yes it is!"

"No, it's not!"

"Whatever." Brandie turned again and started to walk away.

Angela grabbed her shoulder and spun her around. "So I'm not worth it? You can't wait for me to get, I don't know, *comfortable* with all of this?"

Brandie wiped the tears from her eyes roughly. Her nostrils flared. She looked Angela dead in the eyes and said, "Nope." She turned again and headed back towards her school.

Angela stood dumbfounded, blinking quickly, but the picture didn't change. A few cars sped by before she could gather her thoughts.

"Can I at least give you a ride back?" she shouted. She would never offer such a thing to a man who just broke up with her. But Brandie was a woman, and she deserved to be treated like a lady.

"It's only ten blocks!" Brandie yelled over her shoulder. "I think I'll make it!"

Angela shook her head as she watched her first (female) love walk out of her life. The customers at McDonalds were still grinning when she went back to retrieve her car.

Fire joins moon with dark eclipses
Shading portions of the earth
Distant stars collide without witness
Giving way to miraculous births
For each molecule a mate is provided
The seas burst forth as do the skies
Constantly entities are united
Then why not you and I?

CHAPTER SIX
THE FINAL CHAPTER
SOUL CHECK

Angela and Keshaun skipped the gym that Friday. Instead they opted for the football field at Langston Hughes Middle School. It was well lit after dark, and the perimeter fence was never locked. The quarter mile track encircling the field was in great condition. The sun was nearly gone from the sky by the time they got there, but Angela didn't fear for her safety when she was with Keshaun. He was tall and athletic. His powerful leg muscles flexed under his canvas shorts as he jogged alongside his best bud.

They were already a mile into their workout. Neither of them was sweating profusely, but Keshaun's tee shirt clung to the moisture on his pectorals. He was an awesome specimen of a man, but Angela wasn't attracted to him. She didn't think she'd be attracted to anyone, male or female, for the next month or so.

"So, do you think she was right?" Keshaun asked as they ran. His voice was compassionate. Angela looked super sexy in her biker shorts, but Keshaun wasn't a horn-dog tonight. His friend was hurting, and he had nothing but empathy for her.

"About me using her?" Angela asked. She was slightly winded, but not too much. The night air was cool and crisp. It felt good to be outside. It felt good to run and sweat and try to sort things out with someone who had an outside perspective. "Keshaun, I wouldn't do that. I, I don't think I would."

"But you're not sure?"

"It's all really confusing," Angela explained. "I mean, yeah, when I first ran into her, that was the first thought on my mind. Brandie and I got close to experimenting in college, but I backed out. When I saw her again, I wanted to know what it would've been like, if we went all the way. That was my first thought, but that's not all I wanted from her. Is that wrong?"

"I don't think so," Keshaun said. "When I see a fine woman, that's my first thought, too. I'm sexually attracted to her, and I wonder what sex with her would be like."

"But that doesn't mean you get in a relationship just to have sex with her, right?"

"No," Keshaun agreed. "That would be wrong. If I don't like her or want to be with her, then I wouldn't pursue her just for sex. But, to keep it real, I have done that in the past. I met girls who I knew would only be a one night stand. Only you know what you wanted from Brandie."

"I didn't want her just for sex," Angela said definitively.

"Then that's it," Keshaun said. "She's wrong about you. You can't convince her otherwise, so you just have to let her be wrong."

Angela thought about it for a second, and then she frowned. "But, Keshaun, I did want her to be my first experience with a woman. I even told her so."

"That doesn't mean you used her," Keshaun said. "You said you liked her and wanted to be in a relationship."

"I did. I still do. I love how smart she is, and funny. And her strength. There's so much about her that made me think we would be together for a long time. I was falling in love with her."

"Let it go," Keshaun suggested. "You don't use people, Angela. I know you very well. That's not a part of who you are."

Keshaun's words warmed her heart. But overall Angela was still depressed about getting dumped.

"She also said I told her I was ready for a relationship, but it turned out I wasn't."

"Did you tell her that?" Keshaun asked.

"Yeah, I did," Angela said. "But I wasn't lying. I honestly thought I was."

"What changed? What went wrong?"

"I don't think anything went wrong," Angela said. "I think there are two types of ready, and I didn't explain myself well enough."

Keshaun frowned. "Yeah, I can see that, because I have no idea what you're talking about."

Angela grinned at him. "When she asked if I was ready, I said yes. And I was. I was ready to kiss a woman, ready to date a woman, ready to make love to a woman; you know, all of the things I would do with a man."

"But you weren't ready to go public with your new sexuality," Keshaun deduced.

"Exactly. But those are two totally separate things."

Keshaun didn't say anything.

"They are, aren't they?" Angela asked.

"I can see both sides," Keshaun said. "What you say makes sense. But if I was Brandie, and all you said to me was, 'I'm ready to be with you,' then yeah, I can understand why she thinks you lied. You knew she was a lesbian; a hundred percent out of the closet. You know lesbians have public relationships. They don't sneak around and meet at motels. They hold hands and kiss in public. *Technically*, you said you were ready for all of that."

"Oh my God," Angela said. She had a horrible feeling in her gut. "You're right, Keshaun. I did tell her I was ready."

"It's not the end of the world," he said. "You live and learn."

"That's it? Just live and learn? That advice sucks."

He laughed. "Well, if you meet another lesbian woman, then you know what to tell her if she asks if you're ready, right? You know that you have to tell her you're ready for *this*, but not *that*. You have to be specific, so there won't be any misunderstandings later."

Angela nodded. That made perfect sense.

"You do plan on seeing another woman, don't you?" he asked.

"I'm not even thinking–"

"Yeah, blah blah blah," Keshaun said. "Everybody says that shit when they break up with somebody. You know if you still like women or not."

Angela smirked.

Keshaun turned and watched her face while they ran.

"Yep. I can see it in your eyes," he said. "I've been wanting to ask you, since you've been with men and women now... Which one is better?"

Angela smiled. "It's hard to compare."

"Shut the fuck up!" Keshaun broke into laughter. "Why you giving me all these copy and paste answers?"

"It is hard to compare."

"Well, tell me the differences, then."

"Women are soft," Angela mused. She stared at the track ahead of them, but in her mind's eye, she saw Brandie. "They're sweet. Their touch, their smell, it's all different."

"Are women more passionate?"

"I can't say that for sure," Angela said. "'Cause I've been with some *very* passionate men. And I like to be dominated by strong men. I like it when they throw me on the bed and grab my hair and yank my panties off."

"Damn," Keshaun muttered. "A woman can't do all that."

"Some of them can," Angela said.

"Those bull dykes?"

"Stop calling them that."

"What am I supposed to call them?"

"I think they like *stud*."

"You don't know your damned self!" Keshaun said and laughed.

"I know," Angela admitted. "It's a lot I don't know about women who like women."

"Are you going to find out?" Keshaun asked. "Or are you sticking to men from now on?"

"I don't even wanna think about–"

"Cut the bullshit, Angie. I asked you a simple question. You know if you still like women, or if you'll only date men now. I know your ass ain't gonna be celibate."

Angela thought for a few seconds. "The next person who approaches me, male or female, will get rejected," she said. "I'm not ready for any of that mess right now. But when I do decide to date again, I'll be open to a male or a female, if they treat me good, and I'm attracted to them. I do know one thing, though."

"What's that?"

"I will *never* front a man again," Angela said. "You know, I see that all the time; women raising their voice, trying to embarrass their boyfriend in public when they argue. I did it myself a few times. But damn, Keshaun. Now that a girl fronted me out like that, I know how bad it is. I want to apologize for women in general for that awful, awful practice."

Keshaun chuckled, and they finished their second mile with little talking. The sound of their feet clapping the pavement became a rhythm that filled the night air.

When they were done, Keshaun marveled at how beautiful Angela was as she blotted the sweat from her face with a soft towel. With no makeup and her hair held back with a scrunchie, Angela was a 10. Keshaun wanted to hold her and tell her he should be her next man. They were the perfect couple in college and had remained best friends since then.

Angela was the only woman who ever put him in a platonic bubble. Keshaun tolerated it because he loved her. But at times like this, when Angela was suffering from a broken heart, he wanted nothing more than to make love to her until she felt no pain – until she knew that he would always be there for her, and he was all she ever needed.

But now was not the time for such lofty ambitions. Now *never* seemed like a good time, but that didn't mean his day would never come.

TO BE CONTINUED...

BY KEITH THOMAS WALKER

ABOUT THE AUTHOR

Keith Thomas Walker, known as the Master of Romantic Suspense and Urban Fiction, is the author of more than a dozen novels, including *Fixin' Tyrone*, *Dripping Chocolate* and *The Realest Ever*. Keith enjoys reading, poetry and music of all genres. Originally from Fort Worth, Keith is a graduate of Texas Wesleyan University. Visit him at www.keithwalkerbooks.com.